DINOSAUR Land

Double Trouble!

M.J.MISRA

Books in the Dinosaur Land series

The Magic Fossil

Double Trouble!

Lost in the Wild!

The Great Escape!

For Spike, Alfie and Oscar

EGMONT

We bring stories to life

Dinosaur Land: Double Trouble!
First published in Great Britain 2012
by Egmont UK Limited
239 Kensington High Street
London W8 6SA

ISBN 978 1 4052 5940 8

1 3 5 7 9 10 8 6 4 2

www.egmont.co.uk

A CIP catalogue record for this title is available from the British Library

Printed and bound by CPI Group (UK) Ltd, Croydon, CR0 4YY

49334/1

CONTENTS

Magic!

Max Jordan sat on a bale of straw holding his special fossil in his hand. It looked just like a snail shell carved out of grey stone. He ran his fingers over the ridges on it and held his breath.

Nothing happened.

Max heaved a sigh of disappointment.

He had found the fossil on the beach a few weeks ago and taken it home. Later that night it had started to glow, and magically whisked him away to an amazing place called Dinosaur Land, where real dinosaurs lived!

It had been a brilliant adventure, but when he got home and told his mum and dad all about it they hadn't believed him.

Still, Max knew that it *had* happened. It would just be his own special secret. He was really hoping that one day the fossil would take him to Dinosaur Land again.

Max heard a door opening. He put the fossil into his pocket just as his dad came out of a nearby stable.

Max stood up. 'Is Sandy going to be OK?' he asked. His dad was a vet and had been called out to the riding stables to see a sick pony. Max had come with him.

'Yes, she is,' Max's dad replied as the golden-coloured pony put her head over the stable door.

Max went over to stroke her. 'What's the matter with her, Dad?'

'She's got an illness called laminitis,'

Mr Jordan explained. 'She's been eating too much sweet, rich grass and her feet have swollen inside her hooves. They're really hurting her. She should be fine, but she can't have any more grass for a while – just some hay and lots of rest. When she does go back outside it'll have to be into a paddock that doesn't have much grass.'

Max was glad the pony was going to get better. He loved animals almost as much as dinosaurs!

'Are we going to the dentist now?' he asked his dad. He had toothache and they were going to get it checked once they had finished at the stables.

'There's another horse here I need to see first. He's been having terrible trouble eating and I think he might need to have his teeth rasped.'

'Have his teeth rasped?' echoed Max. 'Ouch! That sounds so painful!'

'Don't worry,' said Mr Jordan. 'Horses

6

sometimes get sharp edges on their teeth, which make it uncomfortable for them to eat. They have to be filed down, but it doesn't hurt a bit.' Mr Jordan grinned and took a big metal file out of his bag. It was as long as his forearm. 'I bet you're glad you're not a horse though, Max!' he said, waving it around in the air.

'Very!' said Max, imagining having his teeth filed down.

'Let me just see to this horse and then

we'll go to the dentist,' his dad told him.

Max sat down again with his fossil. He stroked the stone's grey ridges and thought about everything that had happened in Dinosaur Land. He'd met a girl called Fern and her dad, Adam, as well as lots of real, live dinosaurs. Adam looked after the dinosaurs who were sick or unhappy. He was kind of a vet like Max's dad . . . only a dinosaur vet!

I wish I could go back and see them, Max thought longingly.

Suddenly a sharp tingle ran across his fingers. Max looked down and gasped. The fossil was casting out a pale, silvery light. It had shone like this once before . . . when the magic had whisked him to Dinosaur Land.

The light grew brighter and a humming noise filled the air. Max clutched the fossil tightly as a whirling cloud of colours surrounded him.

He felt himself being lifted up and spun around, twisting and turning somersaults . . . until he landed with a sudden bump.

Max opened his eyes and looked about. He could see some tall trees, a lake and a smoking volcano in the distance. His heart leaped.

'Oh, wow!' he breathed. He was back in Dinosaur Land!

Dinosaur Land

Last time Max had visited Dinosaur Land it had been dry and dusty – but it was different now. The land around him was lush and green. It was still extremely hot but there were puddles of rainwater on the floor and plants with big, thick leaves dotted about everywhere. Insects buzzed in the damp air.

Max felt sticky and uncomfortable in his jeans and sweatshirt. He looked over and saw the path leading to Fern and Adam's little white stone house. It was surrounded by ponds and swamps, and paddocks and barns where the sick dinosaurs were kept. A massive, long-necked diplodocus was eating the leaves from some tall trees in one paddock, a spiny-backed stegosaurus was bathing in a swamp and two baby gallimimuses, who looked a little bit

like ostriches, were playing in a pen.

Max's heart thumped with excitement and he set off down the path at a run!

Fern turned in fright as Max burst into the dinosaur sanctuary. Then her face broke into a wide grin.

'Max!' she exclaimed. She brushed her tangle of brown hair off her face and put down the wheelbarrow she was pushing. 'You've come to visit us again!'

'Yes! The magic fossil brought me back!' said Max. He climbed the fence and jumped eagerly into the paddock. A male dinosaur was investigating the food inside the wheelbarrow. It was a plant-eater with a slender neck and a long tail. Its head was small, its dark eyes bright and it wasn't much taller than Fern. *A dryosaurus*, Max thought, recognising it from his dinosaur book back at home.

'Meet Dart,' said Fern, with a smile.

'He's here because he hurt his leg, but he's almost better now.'

'Hello, Dart,' said Max. The dryosaurus stared at him. Max stood very still and held out his hand. The young dinosaur put his head down and approached, his nostrils flaring, his neck stretched out. He sniffed Max's hand. Max gently stroked Dart's rough, scaly face, and the dinosaur pushed his head against Max's arm.

'He likes you!' Fern said happily.

Max grinned at her. It was amazing to be here with the dinosaurs again. If only his mum and dad could see him! 'It's so cool here!' he said, thinking aloud.

'Cool?' Fern said in surprise. 'It's not cool,

it's really hot at the moment.' She looked down at her lightweight cotton tunic and trousers tied with a belt of rope.

Max laughed. ' "Cool" means "good" in my world!'

Fern cocked her head to one side. She looked confused.

'I just meant that it's great to be here,' Max explained.

'Well, I'm really glad you've come back,' Fern told him. 'Hey, I wonder why the magic brought you to us this time?'

Max shrugged. 'Who knows?'

'Hmm. Maybe you've come to help us solve another dinosaur problem!' Fern said, her brown eyes widening.

'I hope so!' Max exclaimed. 'How's Cory?' he asked, thinking about the sweet baby allosaurus he had helped on his first trip to Dinosaur Land.

'He's doing well. We released him into the wild with Rosie and her babies but they stayed quite close so we often see him.'

'Was he old enough to be released?' Max asked, surprised.

Fern nodded. 'Yes, it's been about three months since you were last here.'

'Three months!' Max echoed. 'No way! It's only been two weeks.'

'Not here.' Fern frowned. 'I guess time must pass differently in our worlds. We've been busy! After we released Cory, some new dinosaurs came. And there's been a lot of rain, which is good because it means there's loads of vegetation for the plant-eaters so none of them have been going hungry.' She looked out beyond the sanctuary's paddocks. 'Dad's out at the moment. He's gone to see if there are any dinosaurs in trouble. He's got a new way of travelling.' Her face broke into a grin. 'You're going to love it! I can't wait to show you, but first you'd better come and get changed.' She looked at Max's thick sweatshirt and jeans.

'Your clothes look even stranger than they did last time, and you must be boiling!'

'Hey! My clothes are totally normal!' Max protested.

Fern raised her eyebrows. 'Well, not in Dinosaur Land!' she laughed.

Max followed Fern into her house. It was simple and homely, with basic wooden furniture. Fern found a tunic and trousers for Max. They felt a bit weird but they were definitely more comfortable in the sticky heat. He tied the belt and then rubbed his mouth. His tooth was hurting again.

'Are you all right?' Fern asked, noticing.

'Yeah. I've just got toothache – I've had it for a few days.'

Fern looked thoughtful for a moment, then she went over to a cupboard and pulled it open. There were all sorts of herbs and strange bundles hanging inside. She pulled out a square of brownish green bark and handed it to Max. 'This is willow-wood. It's good for toothache. If you chew on it you'll feel better.'

Max looked at the thin piece of bendy wood. He couldn't imagine his dentist at home giving him bark to chew on! But he put it in his mouth and bit down. It tasted horrible!

Max pulled a face and Fern laughed. 'I know it doesn't taste nice, but it will help, I promise!'

Max really didn't believe her but he chewed hard. To his surprise, after a few minutes, his tooth started to ache less. 'It's feeling a bit better!' he said.

'Told you!' Fern went to the door. 'Let's go. I want to show you the new dinosaurs. Especially Wilfie!'

'Wilfie?' said Max.

Fern's eyes shone. 'Yes. He's one of my favourites.'

Max followed her outside, still chewing the bark. It had softened now and was a bit like very tough chewing gum.

Fern took him round all the pens and introduced him to the injured stegosaurus

28

paddling in the swamp and the two young

gallimimuses whose mother had been killed

by a big T-Rex. They were all plant-eaters.

Max remembered from last time that adult

meat-eaters were never brought into the

sanctuary. They were far too likely to try

and eat the other dinosaurs there! Only gentle plant-eaters and baby meat-eaters were allowed.

The stegosaurus waded out of the swamp and Max scratched its big head. Its eyelids drooped and it sighed happily. 'What do you call a sleeping stegosaurus?' Max said.

'I don't know,' said Fern.

'A stego-SNORE-rus!' grinned Max.

Fern giggled. 'I've missed your jokes! You'll have to tell that one to Dad! Do you know any jokes about bactrosauruses?'

'Nope,' said Max. 'Why?'

'Because Wilfie is a bactrosaurus. Come and meet him!'

They left the stegosaurus and went into a barn.

Wilfie the bactrosaurus was standing on his strong, muscular hind legs, rubbing his horse-like head against the wall.

His front legs were a bit like arms and his body was brown and stripy. Up on his back legs he was about the height of two men, but as he saw Fern and Max come in, he lowered himself down and thudded over. Standing on all fours, his head was just a bit higher than Max's.

Fern hugged him. 'So, here he is. He's really clever, aren't you, Wilfie?' Wilfie rubbed his cheek against her shoulder. 'He likes being stroked!'

Max tickled the friendly dinosaur. Wilfie's eyes blinked at him, bright and alert.

'He's been here since just after you left last time and I've been teaching him to do tricks,' Fern went on. 'Look!' She stepped back and held out a hand. 'Pleased to meet you, Wilfie.'

The bactrosaurus held out his front left leg and Fern shook his foot. Then she fed him a treat from her pocket.

'That's brilliant!' said Max.

'Do you like my friend Max?' Fern said to the dinosaur, nodding her head.

Wilfie copied her, bobbing his own large
head up and down. Fern gave him another
treat. 'Isn't he . . .' She hesitated over the
new word she had learned earlier. 'Cool?'

'Very!' agreed Max. 'Why's he here?'

'Well, he came in because of this wound.' Fern showed Max a scar on Wilfie's side. 'It healed up nicely and Dad was going to release him, but then he stopped eating. We don't know why but he's just gone off his food in the last few weeks.' She turned to the dinosaur. 'He won't eat anything apart from treats and he can't survive on those forever. It's not exactly healthy. We can't release him while he's not eating properly.'

Fern looked really worried.

'What is it that you're giving him?' Max asked curiously.

Fern pulled another treat out of her pocket and showed him. It looked like a chunk of thick, green plant stem. 'It's sugar cane. He loves it, but it's bad for him.'

Wilfie took the piece she offered, but this time he only chewed for a second and then dropped it on the floor. Fern sighed. 'That's not good. He *really* can't be very well if he doesn't even want to eat his favourite thing. Oh, Wilfie.' She hugged him tight. 'You've got to start eating properly.'

Max stroked the dinosaur. His forehead wrinkled as he tried to think what could be wrong. 'What does your dad think the problem is?'

'He hasn't a clue,' Fern said sadly.

'I wish I could help,' said Max.

Fern gasped and her eyes widened. 'Maybe you can! Oh, Max! Perhaps that's why you've come here again – to help find out what's wrong with Wilfie!'

Travelling by Dinosaur!

Max stared at Fern. Was she right? Had the magic fossil brought him to Dinosaur Land to help with the sick bactrosaurus?

Well, I helped them last time, Max reminded himself. *Maybe I can help again.*

'So, has your dad tried lots of different foods?' he asked.

'Yes. We've tried all kinds of grass, ferns and leaves. It's just so strange because bactrosauruses are usually greedy and will eat most things.'

Max looked at Wilfie. The dinosaur looked back at him hopefully, almost as if he was willing him to help. He rubbed his head against Max again. Max stroked him, thinking hard.

Just then they heard a shout outside.

'Fern!'

'Dad's back!' Fern said. 'Come on – let's go and tell him you're here.'

They patted Wilfie goodbye, then left the barn and shut the door behind them. Adam, Fern's dad, was at the entrance to the sanctuary. Max stared. He couldn't believe his eyes! Adam was sitting on the back of a brown and green dinosaur. It looked similar to a triceratops; its body was shaped a bit like a rhinoceros, with four sturdy legs, a long tail, a large frill at the back of its head and two horns sticking up towards the sky. Its third horn was on the end of its nose and curved downwards. It was wearing a simple bridle, reins leading from a bit in its mouth. Adam was sitting where the dinosaur's neck joined its body.

Fern grinned from ear to ear at Max's astonished expression. 'I told you Dad had found a new way to travel!'

'Max!' Adam shouted over in delight. 'Welcome back!'

'Isn't it great!' said Fern. 'He's going to try and help us work out what's wrong with Wilfie.'

'Excellent!' Her father beamed. 'Now, why don't you hop on board? I've spotted a herd of edmontonias over to the west and I want to check them out. They don't look quite right to me. Maybe you can help me with those too!'

Fern grabbed Max's hand and they ran over together.

'Down, Trixie,' Fern's dad said to the dinosaur. Trixie kneeled so her shoulders were just above Max's head. Adam jumped off. 'You two can ride. I'll walk for a bit.' He helped Max on and then Fern behind him. Max patted Trixie's rough neck. 'What type of dinosaur is she?' He'd never seen one quite like her. 'She's not a triceratops,' he said. 'She's too small and her nose horn curves a different way.'

'Well spotted,' said Adam. 'It would be

45

easy to get them confused, but you're right
– Trixie is actually an einiosaurus.'

'I-nee-oh-saw-rus.' Max copied the way
Adam said the name. Excitement fizzed
through him. He knew his dinosaur fact
book off by heart and he had thought he
knew about every kind of dinosaur there
was. It was brilliant to meet a new type of
dinosaur that he *hadn't* heard of.

'She's very gentle,' said Adam. 'And
she's taken well to giving rides. She's just

the right build for it and she seems to like it. Now, come on, let's go and find those edmontonias!'

They set off through the lush grass, heading west, with Max holding Trixie's reins and steering as if she was a horse.

'I really hope you do have some good ideas for how to help Wilfie,' Adam said to Max. 'I'm so worried about him. He can't survive on treats forever!'

Max longed to help. He thought about the animals his parents treated. They often saw cats and dogs and horses who had gone off their food. Max remembered a dog that

had come in a while ago. It had swallowed some chicken bones and its stomach hurt so much that it couldn't eat.

'It might not be the food that's the problem. There could easily be something else that's stopping Wilfie from eating,' Max said slowly.

'Hmm, I have checked him all over,' said Adam, 'and he seems fine. No runny nose, no sensitive tummy or cough. But I'll take another look at him when we get back. Maybe he does have a virus or something.'

Fern pointed to the left, where a large dinosaur with a duck-like bill and a crest was leading her baby across the plain. 'Look, there's a maiasaura and her pup, Max.'

Max thought of a another joke he knew. 'What has a headcrest, a bill and sixteen wheels?'

Fern shrugged. 'What?' she said.

'A maiasaura on roller skates!' said Max.

Fern and Adam looked at each other with puzzled expressions.

'Roller skates go on your feet,' said Max. 'They've got little wheels and you can whizz around on them really fast.'

Now Fern and Adam looked even more confused. 'But why would you want to do that?' asked Adam.

Max shook his head. 'It doesn't matter. It's hard to explain!' He grinned.

Adam smiled back. 'Your world sounds very different to ours.'

'Oh, it is,' said Max.

'Let's see if you get one of *our* jokes,' said Adam. He winked at Fern. 'What's the best

52

way to talk to a T-Rex?'

Max did know the answer to that one. 'Long distance!' he exclaimed.

Adam chuckled. 'Right first time.' Then he pointed over their heads. 'Hey! Look over there – it's the edmontonias!'

Max looked and saw six edmontonias standing among some low shrubs and grass. They were quite a distance away but even so he could see why Adam had wanted to investigate. The way they were standing was strange. They had rocked back their tank-like bodies to take the weight off their hoof-like claws. They looked very uncomfortable and miserable, and not one of them was eating.

'I don't like the look of that,' said Adam anxiously. 'Here, let me get on Trixie with you. We need to get over there as quickly as possible.'

Max pulled the reins and Trixie stopped. 'Down, girl!' Max said. Trixie kneeled and

Adam jumped on behind Fern. The strong
dinosaur could easily carry them all.

'Time to speed up,' said Adam as Trixie stood. 'Hold on tight!' He slapped his hand behind his leg. 'Come on, Trixie, my beauty. Off we go!'

The dinosaur broke into a lolloping run. Her back swayed from side to side like a boat in a stormy sea. Max clung to her neck for dear life. He'd never experienced anything like this before!

Fern squealed. 'Dad!' She grabbed Max's waist. 'We're going to fall off!'

Adam laughed behind them. 'No you're not! Just keep hanging on tight!'

They sped across the plain and Max felt exhilaration flood through him. They passed a pack of lambeosauruses which leaped forwards and sprinted after them. Soon they were racing neck to neck.

'Whoa! We had better slow down!' Max panted, looking at all the lambeosauruses stampeding around them. But Trixie just went faster!

After a while, the lambeosauruses fell back, but Trixie kept on going until she reached the edmontonias.

As she slowed to a lumbering walk, Max felt like he had been on the bounciest, jerkiest theme-park ride ever.

'That was amazing!' he said as Trixie finally stopped.

'Much better than walking!' said Fern.

'And we got to the edmontonias quicker,' said Adam. 'Down, girl!' he called to Trixie.

She kneeled and they all climbed off.

The poor edmontonias looked at them sorrowfully. Their humped, spiky backs were about as tall as Adam's head, but their own heads hung low to the ground. They didn't move. All of them were leaning back on their heels. One of them made a low bellowing sound.

'Oh dear,' said Adam. 'They're not happy. They're not happy at all.'

The Edmontonias

'What's the matter with them, Dad?' Fern asked, looking at the sad edmontonias. 'Why are they standing like that? They look like they don't want to put any weight on their front claws.'

Adam's forehead wrinkled. 'I'm not sure, but I've seen something like this before.

A few years ago when we had a lot of rain,

some of the plant-eaters got sore feet.'

'Laminitis!' Max burst out, remembering

the pony his dad had been treating at the stables. 'It's something ponies get in my world. My dad told me that when they eat too much sweet, new grass their feet swell up inside their hooves.' He looked at the dinosaurs. 'It could be the same with the edmontonias – their claws are a bit like hooves.'

'Of course!' Fern gasped. 'There's been lots of rich grazing for them because of all the rain.'

'You've got to stop them eating it,' Max said. 'Feed them dry hay or something like that instead.'

'Brilliant!' said Adam, clapping him on the back. 'I'm very glad you came today, Max. I'm sure you must be right. So . . .' He glanced back at the six edmontonias. 'Let's get them back to the sanctuary.'

'How are we going to do that, Dad?' said Fern. She looked at Max but he was baffled too. You couldn't exactly lead a group of dinosaurs like a troupe of ponies!

Adam grinned. 'We'll round them up of course. We'll use Trixie to herd them back to the sanctuary!' He patted Trixie. 'It'll mean some more cantering though!'

'Hooray!' Max and Fern both cried.

Adam sat at the front this time so he could hold the reins and steer, while Fern and Max clung on behind him. Trixie shuffled around the edmontonias. At first they threw their heads in the air, reluctant to move, but as she came closer to them they gradually started to lollop across the plain.

'Yee-haa!' shouted Adam, waving a rope that he had been carrying round his waist. It was like being a cowboy – only they were rounding up dinosaurs instead of cows!

Gradually, Max got used to Trixie's canter and managed to sit straight. 'They're going the right way!' he shouted as the edmontonias headed towards the sanctuary.

'I'm going to put them in the East Barn,' Adam called over his shoulder to Fern. He herded the edmontonias right round the outskirts of the sanctuary towards a big stone building.

'Whoa!' he called to Trixie. She stopped. 'OK, you two, can you run and open the doors and help me get them in there? We don't want them going round the outside.'

Fern and Max nodded and jumped down. Now that Trixie had stopped, the edmontonias had too. They were looking around curiously at the pens and buildings. Fern and Max raced past them to the big double doors of the barn. It took both of them to heave the doors open, one at a time.

'Now to get them in!' said Fern. 'Maybe I should use some sugar cane to tempt them.'

'No,' Max said quickly. 'It will just make their feet hurt more. We'll have to try and get them in without treats.'

Adam had begun herding the dinosaurs

towards the barn. The ground shuddered as their feet stomped across it. It felt as if a herd of elephants was approaching!

Suddenly the lead edmontonia gave an alarmed snort and tried to head round the side of the barn. It seemed to be scared of going inside. Fern ran towards it, waving and shouting, cutting off its path. But the dinosaur took no notice and kept on lumbering towards her. It was going to run her over!

Max ran to join Fern. 'Go the other way!' he yelled at the edmontonias, waving his arms and jumping up and down. The leading dinosaur stopped. It eyed them warily then shuffled round and tried to go past the barn the other way. Adam was waiting on that side, still on Trixie's back.

The head edmontonia ground to a halt

again and looked back
at the open barn doors.

Fern, Max and Adam
advanced on both
sides. With another
snort, the dinosaur
walked inside. The rest
of the herd followed it.

'Hooray!' Fern cheered.

'Way to go!' said Max, holding up his
hand in a high five. He had tried to teach

Fern how to do them on his last visit. She grinned and remembered to slap his palm with her own.

'High five!'

'Good teamwork!' said Adam as he dismounted Trixie and shut the barn doors before the edmontonias could come out. 'OK, I'll go and fetch them some hay and some herbs to help with the pain. If you're right, Max, they should start to get better in a few days. We'll try and make them as comfortable as possible then I'll turn them out into one of the dust paddocks where there's only a little grass. They can go back to the wild when the vegetation dies down.

You've been a really big help today, Max!'

'I just hope I can help Wilfie too,' said Max with a frown.

Max and Fern helped Adam to cart ten wheelbarrows of hay into the barn, then Adam went to find the herbs that would ease the edmontonias' painful hooves.

'Let's go and see Wilfie,' said Fern when the edmontonias were happily munching on their hay.

'OK,' agreed Max.

They set off. Poor Wilfie was standing quietly in his barn, his head hanging low. He was drooling slightly.

'Oh, Wilfie, you really don't look happy,' said Fern.

The bactrosaurus pushed his head into her side and groaned.

Fern offered him a piece of sugar cane. Wilfie took it but dropped it from his mouth on the first chew.

Max watched carefully. It looked like

Wilfie was having real problems chewing. Suddenly something else his dad had said at the stables came flooding back to him. 'Maybe his teeth hurt when he chews!' Max exclaimed. 'That could be what's wrong. His teeth might need rasping!' He saw Fern's puzzled look. 'A rasp is a big metal file that smooths down sharp edges on a horse's teeth so they don't hurt when it tries to eat.'

Fern started to frown. 'But, Max . . .'

'No, I really think that's it!' said Max, fired up by his success with the edmontonias. 'Come on! Let's go and tell your dad!'

Max raced back to the East Barn without waiting for Fern. He found Adam carrying

buckets of water for the edmontonias to drink. 'Guess what, Adam! I think I know what's wrong with Wilfie. And it's not a stomach ache or virus!' Max's eyes shone as the words tumbled from his mouth. When he finished explaining, he looked eagerly at Adam. 'Don't you think that could be what's wrong? You could make a metal file and rasp his teeth!'

Fern had run up beside him. Max saw her exchange looks with her dad.

'I'm not sure you're right this time, Max,' said Adam. 'You see, bactrosauruses like Wilfie are part of a group of dinosaurs called hadrosaurs. They have lots of teeth at the back of their mouths but they constantly grow new ones and the old ones fall out. Their teeth don't stay in their mouths long enough to get sharp edges.'

'Oh, yes. Of course.' Max felt as if one of Adam's buckets of cold water had been poured over him. He *knew* that hadrosaurs had teeth like that – he'd read about it lots of times. And he should have realised that bactrosauruses like Wilfie were part of the hadrosaur family. He just hadn't stopped to

think about it properly because he'd been
so sure he was right! Max's cheeks went red.

'Sorry . . . it was a really stupid idea.'

Adam saw Max's expression and smiled

kindly. 'Not stupid. You can't be expected to know everything about *all* dinosaurs. Even I don't. Each time you've been here I've learned something from you, and I've been looking after dinosaurs all my life . . .'

'But I did know about hadrosaurs' teeth,' said Max, still feeling cross with himself. 'I should have remembered.'

'At least you *had* an idea, even if it was the wrong one,' said Adam. 'And . . .' he chuckled, 'I have to say, I'm rather glad you were wrong this time. I wouldn't fancy rasping a dinosaur's teeth, would you?'

Max managed a smile. 'No, I guess not.'

'Especially if it was a T-Rex!' said Fern with a grin.

'What did the dentist say when the dinosaur walked in?' Max said, cheering up a bit as he thought of the joke.

'What's a dentist?' asked Fern.

'It's someone who checks humans' teeth to make sure they're healthy,' replied Max.

'So, what did the dentist say?'

Fern thought for a second. 'I give up!' she said. 'What *did* the dentist say?'

'ARGH!' Max yelled.

They all laughed.

'Let's go back to Wilfie,' said Fern.

'Will you help me fill up the trough with clean water first?' asked Adam. 'Six edmontonias are going to drink quite a lot!'

Fern and Max set about helping him fill the buckets with water from the well.

As Max turned the well's handle, a picture of Wilfie's face swam into his mind. So, the dinosaur didn't need his teeth rasping. But what *was* wrong with him? He really had to find out!

What is wrong with Wilfie?

When the trough was full, Max and Fern went back to check on the bactrosaurus. He plodded to the door when he saw them. Fern hugged him. 'What is the matter with you, Wilfie?'

Wilfie rubbed his head against Fern's shoulder and then looked at her intently with his dark eyes. It was as though he was trying to tell them what was wrong. Max wished dinosaurs could talk.

'Let's get him some food just in case he does want it,' said Fern.

They fetched some grass from the big feeding barn. Wilfie came over to them, but just as he was about to take a bite he seemed to change his mind. He shuffled to the back of the barn.

Max frowned. He looked at the bits of

sugar cane on the floor and then at the way Wilfie was holding his head to one side. Maybe Wilfie didn't need his teeth rasping, but Max couldn't shake off the feeling that there was something wrong with his teeth or mouth.

The air was getting hotter and stickier so Fern suggested that they go back to the house to get something to eat and drink.

'Good idea,' said Max. 'Maybe I'll be able to think more clearly out of this heat.'

The little house was lovely and cool. Fern opened a cupboard that was built into the dirt floor and took out a stone bottle. 'Home-made star fruit and grass cordial,' she said. 'Do you want some?'

Max nodded. He had no idea what it

would taste like but he was feeling very thirsty! Fern poured the sparkling drink out into stone cups. Max tasted it. 'Yum! It's delicious!' he said.

'Dad makes it,' said Fern with a smile. 'Do you want a honey biscuit too?'

She opened another cupboard in the wall and took out a plate of biscuits. She offered one to Max. He took one but as he bit into it, he felt a sharp pain in his tooth. 'Ow!' His hand went to his mouth.

'You need some more willow-wood,' said
Fern. She fetched him a small piece and he
chewed on it. It still tasted bitter but at least
it made his tooth feel better.

'So, why have you got toothache?' she asked him.

Max sighed. 'Dad says it's because I eat too many sweets.'

'Sweets? What are they?'

Max couldn't believe she didn't know what sweets were. 'Sweet things. Some are chewy, some you suck. They're sugary, like. . .' He frowned, trying to work out how he could explain it to her. 'Like the sugar cane Wilfie loves.' He stared at her, his eyes widening. 'Of course!' An idea had just flashed into his head. 'That could be what's wrong with Wilfie!'

'What?' said Fern, confused.

'Maybe he's got toothache!'

'Toothache?'

'Yes!' It was all suddenly making sense to Max. 'You've been feeding him all that sugar cane as you taught him tricks. I bet it's rotting his teeth and making them sore, just like me eating too many sweets! He keeps rubbing his cheek and holding his head on one side and dropping his food. It must be hurting him to eat!

Fern grabbed his hand. 'Oh, Max! Let's go and see if you're right!'

They raced back to the barn. 'Wilfie, we need to see inside your mouth!' Fern said as Wilfie nuzzled her. She put her hands on either side of his jaw and tried to coax it open. 'Come on, let me see.'

But Wilfie pulled his head away from her and plodded over to the far corner.

Fern went after him. She took hold of his mouth again but he snorted and stood up on his hind legs so she couldn't reach him.

'Wilfie!'

But the dinosaur just turned his back on her and swished his long tail.

'What are we going to do?' Fern cried. 'We can't see if he has toothache without looking in his mouth.'

Max stared up at the dinosaur. 'How do you get a dinosaur to open its mouth when it doesn't want to?' He knew lots of dinosaur facts but none of them helped with this!

'It's impossible!' said Fern, shaking her head in despair.

Max stared as Wilfie began shaking his head too. A thought slowly began to form in his brain. 'Fern, nod your head.'

Looking surprised, Fern nodded.

Wilfie copied her.

'That's it!' Max gasped. 'That's how we get him to open his mouth. You've taught him to copy you! Give him a treat and open your mouth.'

Fern looked at him as if he'd gone mad.

'Do it! Try!' Max exclaimed.

Turning to Wilfie, Fern offered him some sugar cane. The dinosaur lowered his head but didn't take the treat. Fern opened her mouth. Wilfie studied her for a moment, then he opened his mouth too.

'It worked!' said Max in delight. 'Keep your mouth open!'

Fern rolled her eyes at him. She couldn't speak. Max went over to Wilfie. 'It's OK,' he murmured. 'I'm not going to hurt you. I just need to look at your teeth.'

He pretended to look in Fern's mouth and then turned to face Wilfie again. The bactrosaurus stood still as Max peered into his jaws. Max could see the brand new teeth pushing the old ones out. Every tooth was really big and long. Max swallowed and tried not to feel too nervous. 'Don't shut your mouth!' he muttered to Fern.

Fern rolled her eyes again but she kept her mouth open as wide as possible.

'There!' Max exclaimed. He had spotted the tooth that was causing the problems. It was near the back and had turned grey. A new tooth was growing underneath the rotten one. In a few days the diseased one would fall out. Max stepped away from the

dinosaur's open jaws. 'It's OK, you can shut

your mouth now, Fern.'

Fern breathed a sigh of relief and shut

her mouth with a snap. Wilfie did the same.

'So what did you see?' Fern asked.

'One of his teeth is rotting,' said Max.

'But dinosaurs never have rotten teeth,' she said, puzzled.

'I guess Wilfie wouldn't normally eat nearly as much sugar as he is here,' said Max. 'He might have a sweet tooth, but he'd usually be out in the wild, eating plants and grass and healthy things.'

Fern looked very guilty. 'Oh, poor Wilfie! And I thought I was being kind.' She bit her lip. 'What can we do to help him?'

'Don't worry. I think the bad tooth is

about to fall out,' said Max. 'It'll probably only be a few days and when it does drop out his toothache will disappear and he'll start eating again. Maybe we can feed him some willow-wood until then to take away the pain. It helped me!'

'Brilliant idea!' cried Fern. She beamed. 'Oh, Max. You're amazing. Thank you!'

Max grinned. 'I'm just glad Wilfie's going to be OK. And you helped too! If you hadn't trained him, we'd never have got his mouth open and found out what was wrong.'

Wilfie came and nuzzled Fern. 'You'll get better soon,' she said, hugging him. 'It's going to be all right.'

The Magic Fossil Glows

Max and Fern went to find Adam and tell him what they had discovered. He was astonished.

'I'd never have thought of a dinosaur getting toothache. It's very lucky you came here today, Max. Thank you for everything you've done.'

'The fossil *did* bring you here to help us,' said Fern. 'I knew it!'

'I hope I can come again,' said Max, taking the fossil out of his pocket.

'Me too – although I suppose that would mean we'd have another problem on our hands! But hopefully Wilfie's toothache will have gone by the time you come back,' said Fern. 'And the edmontonias will have recovered and be back out in the wild.'

'You're so lucky to live here,' said Max,

looking round the sanctuary at all the amazing dinosaurs. It reminded him a bit of his own house with the vet surgery attached and suddenly he felt homesick. He loved Dinosaur Land but he couldn't wait to see his mum and dad again.

A tingle shot across his fingers. He looked down. The fossil was glowing with a silvery light. 'Look, Fern! I think I'm going home!' he gasped.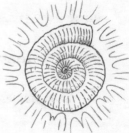

'Oh, wow! It really is magic!

Come back soon!' called Fern.

A whirling cloud of colour swept out of the fossil and surrounded Max. The last thing he saw was Fern and Adam smiling and waving at him and then he was whisked away.

Max tumbled round and round, then the cloud cleared and he felt the ground under him. He blinked. He was back at the stables, wearing his own clothes – and it looked like no time had passed at all! Sandy, the pony with laminitis, was looking over her

stable door. She looked very small suddenly compared to the dinosaurs. Max stood up. His head was spinning. It was all so much to take in. He looked at the magic fossil in his hand.

'Hey, Max!' His dad came out of a stable. 'Will you give me a hand?'

'OK,' said Max, slipping the fossil into his pocket.

'Thanks. As soon as I've rasped this horse's teeth I'll take you to the dentist.'

Max groaned inside. He'd had quite enough of teeth for one day!

He remembered his new joke. 'Hey, Dad,' he said, going over. 'What did the dentist say when he saw the dinosaur?'

'What?' said Mr Jordan.

'ARGH!' said Max.

Mr Jordan grinned and shook his head. 'You and your dinosaur jokes. I've never known anyone as dinosaur mad as you. It's a pity you can't meet a real one.'

Max hid his own smile. If only his dad knew! 'Yeah,' he said, touching the magic fossil in his pocket. A warm glow spread through him. 'I guess it is.'

How do you measure up to your favourite dinosaurs?

Tyrannosaurus 4m tall and 13m long

The tyrannosaurus (also known as the T-Rex!) was one of the largest and scariest meat-eaters around. It had massive teeth, and its head was so big it could have eaten a human in one bite!

Pterodactyl wingspan of 1.5m

Pterodactyls had big wings, but they didn't have feathers. They were probably furry, like bats!

Gallimimus
2m tall and 6-8m long

The gallimimus had a small head, large eyes and no teeth. It was shaped like a huge ostrich. It was clever and a very fast runner, so if a tyrannosaur turned up it didn't stick around!

Bactrosaurus 2m tall and 6m long

The bactrosaurus had a beak shaped a bit like a duck's bill. It was smaller than a lot of plant-eating dinosaurs but it still weighed as much as a car!

Stegosaurus 3-4m tall and 9m long

The stegosaurus was much bigger than a human, but its brain was only the size of a walnut! It definitely wasn't the cleverest dinosaur around . . .

Edmontonia 2m tall and 6-7m long

The edmontonia was covered in bony plates. The plates protected the dinosaur from predators, like armour. It had spines on its neck and shoulders, which might have been used to shove other dinosaurs out of the way!

Allosaurus 5m tall and 8.5m long

The allosaurus was a very big, meat-eating dinosaur. It had sharp teeth that were up to ten centimetres long and it was very clever. It didn't have much trouble catching its lunch!

Lambeosaurus
2-3m tall and 10-15m long

The lambeosaurus had a crest on the top of its head and a beak similar to the bactrosaurus. It weighed as much as five elephants!

EGMONT PRESS: ETHICAL PUBLISHING

Egmont Press is about turning writers into successful authors and children into passionate readers – producing books that enrich and entertain. As a responsible children's publisher, we go even further, considering the world in which our consumers are growing up.

Safety First
Naturally, all of our books meet legal safety requirements. But we go further than this; every book with play value is tested to the highest standards – if it fails, it's back to the drawing-board.

Made Fairly
We are working to ensure that the workers involved in our supply chain – the people that make our books – are treated with fairness and respect.

Responsible Forestry
We are committed to ensuring all our papers come from environmentally and socially responsible forest sources.

For more information, please visit our website at
www.egmont.co.uk/ethicalpublishing